my first
100
ANIMALS

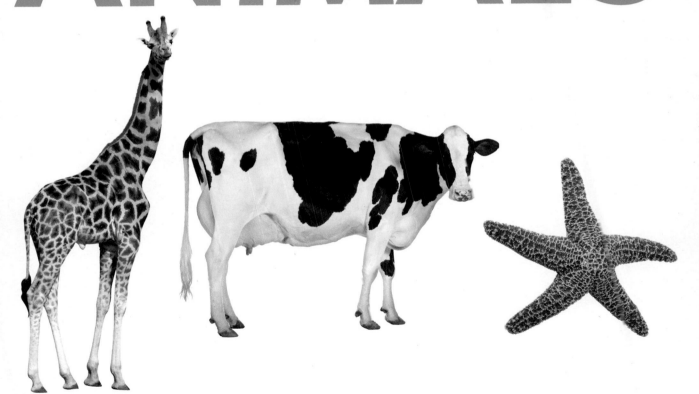

pets & farm animals

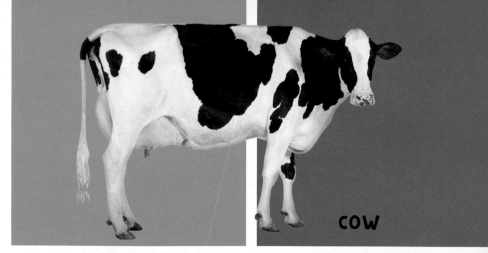

cow

dog

guinea pig

goldfish

goat

cat

rabbit

donkey

yak

bull

horse

turkey

rooster

camel

birds

peacock

goose

duck

hummingbird

kingfisher

ostrich

flamingo

swan

sparrow

crow

vulture

pigeon

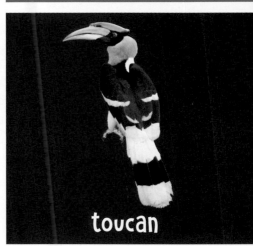

toucan

woodpecker

eagle

parrot

wild animals

panda

bear

zebra

giraffe

kangaroo

fox

gorilla

hyena

tiger

lion

monkey

wolf

elephant

sea animals

dolphin

starfish

pilot whale

clownfish

crab

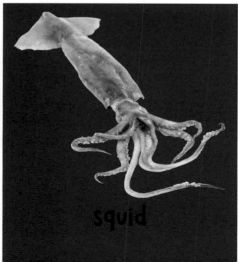
squid

shark

tuna

jellyfish

sea turtle

seahorse

octopus

stingray

lobster

polar animals

arctic tern

snow goose

moose

skua

puffin

snowy owl

reindeer

seal

husky

arctic fox

polar bear

walrus

penguin

baby animals

tiger cub

kitten

lion cub

owlet

parrot chick

kit

kid

penguin chick

chick

duckling

deer fawn

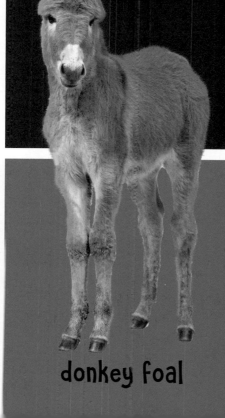

donkey foal

polar bear
cub

bear cub

nocturnal animals

raccoon

bat

otter

ferret

lynx

owl

reptiles & amphibians

chameleon

komodo dragon

crocodile

snake

alligator

frog

garden animals

ladybug

grasshopper

dragonfly

ant

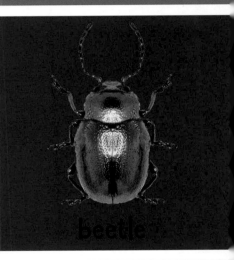

beetle

butterfly

snail

spider